To my little friend
Nelly

Will you be my friend?

Written and Illustrated by
Linda Di Sante

Nelly the cat moved in today and scampered outside wanting to play.

She searched high and low
for a friend or two
but wandered around
with nothing to do.

She roamed through the garden,

gazed up in the trees,

peered into the bushes,

even under the peas!

Lonely and blue,
Nelly started to cry.
*There's no one to play
with — not even a fly!*

She sat in sad silence,
but something had stirred!
So she lifted her head
and that's when she heard,

Will you be my friend?
sang a bird in the tree.
I have always been told
I'm as nice as can be!

A spinning spider
swung from her web
to say, *A friend is just
what I needed today.*

Two honeybees glanced
up from their meal.
Can we be friends too?
— *Now <u>that's</u> a sweet deal!*

Fuzzy skunk appeared asking,
You know what I think?
When I find a friend,
I don't make a stink!

Slithering through the grass
to hear, squiggly snake hissed,

Oh, having a friend
is ever _ssssoooo_ dear!

Then blind mole poked his
nose from out the ground.
*The words, "be my friend,"
are <u>my</u> favorite sound!*

What about me?
Tiny mouse asked of us.
I can scurry and squeak
and I won't make a fuss!

But <u>can</u> we be friends?
Nelly the cat had to say.
We're so different in looks
— just <u>how</u> do we play?

Let's pretend I am you,
and you are me.

I will _meeeoow_, chirped the bird.
You can sing in the tree!

I will *spin*, said the mouse.
Now watch me, it's fun!

So blind mole began squeaking
as he blinked in the sun.

Fuzzy skunk squirmed and slithered.
Squiggly snake tried to stink.
And the spider and bees
didn't know what to think!

They giggled and danced
and spun all around.

And when they grew tired,
flopped back on the ground.

So Nelly the cat moved in today
and met some new friends who
wanted to stay.
Though each one was different,
they liked to pretend.
And, yes, they *really* were all the
same in the end — *FRIENDS!*

Nelly

17140385R00020

Made in the USA
Middletown, DE
08 January 2015